S0-DQZ-198

by Tim S. Vasquez

illustrated by Linda Kay Ost

Toodaloo Publishing Company
Gilbert, Arizona

Toodaloo Publishing Company
Tim S. Vasquez, President
ivasquez@someburros.com
TheTacoStandBook.com

Publisher's Cataloging-In-Publication Data

Names: Vasquez, Tim S., 1975- author. | Ost, Linda Kay, illustrator.
Title: The taco stand / by Tim S. Vasquez ; illustrated by Linda Kay Ost.
Description: Gilbert, Arizona : Toodaloo Publishing Company, [2019] | Interest age level: 004-010. | Includes Spanish glossary. | Summary: "Isabel loves to make her "famous tacos" for her family and friends. Every morning, her two young sons take the extra tacos she prepares to sell at a homemade stand on Central Avenue in Phoenix. One day, the boys are approached by the man in the black suit who has big business plans for the tacos. Isabel and her family have a big decision to make."--Provided by publisher.
Identifiers: ISBN 9781732647206
Subjects: LCSH: Tacos--Juvenile fiction. | Street-food vendors--Arizona--Phoenix--Juvenile fiction. | Family-owned business enterprises--Arizona--Phoenix--Juvenile fiction. | Families--Arizona--Phoenix--Juvenile fiction. | CYAC: Tacos--Fiction. | Street vendors--Arizona--Phoenix--Fiction. | Family-owned business enterprises--Arizona--Phoenix--Fiction. | Family life--Fiction.
Classification: LCC PZ7.1.V399 Ta 2019 | DDC [Fic]--dc23

Printed in the United States of America
10 9 8 7 6 5 4 3 2 1

This book was produced by Story Monsters LLC.

Cover Design: Jeff Yesh
Illustrations: Linda Kay Ost
Editor: Conrad J. Storad
Proofreaders: Ruthann Raitter and Cristy Bertini
Project Manager: Patti Crane

Dedicated to my Nana and Tata
who showed me the importance of
hard work and the value of family.

ISABEL loved to get up every morning before dawn. She enjoyed sitting in her kitchen to watch the beautiful Arizona sunrise as she sipped her coffee. She sat peacefully and looked around her tiny house in her little old neighborhood. Isabel felt so fortunate for everything she had. She was grateful for her husband, Poncho, and for her two adorable little boys, Ralphie and Georgie.

Isabel looked forward to another warm summer day as she began cooking breakfast for her family. Isabel was an excellent cook! She loved to bring enjoyment to others through her cooking.

Every morning she prepared a delicious breakfast for Poncho and the boys. She cooked chorizo, huevos rancheros, rice, beans, and her "famous tacos." Isabel's tacos were famous because EVERYBODY in town loved them.

She made each "famous taco" with savory shredded beef packed neatly into a soft corn tortilla. Each taco was then lightly fried to a golden brown. She carefully topped each one with grated cheese, crisp shredded lettuce, and fresh chopped tomatoes.

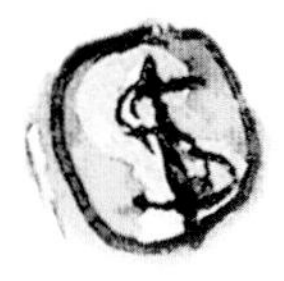

After breakfast was complete, Isabel always made a few dozen extra tacos for her boys to sell on the street corner. The boys set up their homemade stand each day on Central Avenue. Within minutes, a long line of customers would form. The people had money in hand and each hoped they were early enough to get some of the wonderful tacos.

Sale
Central Ave
Isabel's TACOS
I ♥ TACOS
Isabel's Famous TACOS FOR SAL
25¢

When the last taco was sold, the boys proudly took the money home to their mamá and papá. It was never a lot of money, but it was enough to help buy food and new clothes. The boys were always very happy to help the family.

At home, the boys enjoyed spending afternoons playing baseball in the yard with Poncho. Other neighborhood boys would join the games as well. Isabel sat on her front porch and watched with a contented smile on her face.

When the sun went down each day, Isabel headed back to her kitchen to prepare a Mexican feast. Every evening she cooked a delicious meal for her family. They often invited friends to join them at the dinner table. Together, family and friends dined on tacos, enchiladas, tamales, and fresh, homemade tortillas.

The family enjoyed these meals with their friends. They ate, drank, told stories, and laughed late into the night. Isabel loved to cook for other people. Everyone loved the food she made. Her heart was full.

At night, as she tucked Ralphie and Georgie into bed, she thought about what a wonderful day it had been. She thought about how she could not wait to do it all over again the next day.

Isabel was up early the next morning, as usual. The family ate every bite of another delicious breakfast. The boys again set up their taco stand on Central Avenue. And once again, people lined up around the block hoping to buy one of Isabel's "famous tacos."

This morning the boys noticed a new customer in line. He was a man they had never seen before. The stranger wore a fancy black business suit and shiny black shoes. As the man took the first big bite of his delicious taco, the boys watched his eyes light up with happiness. He devoured it in amazement.

When he finished, the man in the black suit looked around. He stared at all the people waiting in line for tacos with money in hand. His eyes lit up again. This time he had an idea.

The man in the black suit walked up to the boys as they closed up their stand for the morning. He asked them if they always had this many people wanting to buy the tacos.

"Si, Señor!" said Georgie.

“These ‘famous tacos’ are mouthwatering! I can’t seem to get enough,” said the man in the suit. “I must know who made them.”

“Mi mamá, Isabel,” Ralphie replied. “She makes the tacos every morning. They are our secret family recipe.”

“Well then, I must meet your mother immediately!” demanded the man in the suit.

“Mi mamá will be busy watching us play ball in the yard this afternoon,” Ralphie said. “But tonight she is cooking a feast at sunset like she does every night. You can join us for dinner and talk to her then, Señor.”

The man in the black suit thanked the boys and gave them each a silver coin for speaking to him.

The man in the black suit arrived at Isabel's house that evening. He was greeted warmly by the entire family. Before dinner was ready, family and guests sat in the family room. Everyone gathered around Poncho as he strummed his guitar. He sang, "La cucaracha, la cucaracha. Ya no puede caminar."

After a few songs, dinner was ready. Everyone sat down at the table to enjoy Isabel's spread of delicious food.

The man in the black suit did not say a word. He dug right in and shoveled bite after bite of the tasty food into his mouth. The only sound he made was, *"Mmmm. Mmmmm. Mmmmmm."*

When the man in the black suit finally finished eating, Isabel politely asked him what he wanted to speak to her about.

"Big business, Isabel. I want to talk to you about BIG, BIG, business," the man said.

"Well, Señor, I'm not sure about that, but go ahead," Isabel replied. "After all, you are our guest."

The man in the suit began to speak. The words flew out of his mouth almost as quickly as he gobbled every bite of his food.

"Well, after tasting your delicious cooking, and after seeing the dozens of people standing in line for your 'famous tacos,' it hit me! I need to benefit from this!" he said with gusto.

"Isabel, I know you enjoy getting up early and cooking breakfast for your family. But think about this," the man said, speaking faster with each sentence. "Instead, what if you woke up earlier and made even more of your 'famous tacos?' Your boys would have more tacos to sell at their stand on the street corner. The more tacos they sell, the more money we make!"

Isabel replied, “But, Señor, I really do love to cook breakfast for my boys. And why would we need any more money? We have everything we need right here in our little home.”

“It’s OK. I see you don’t get it,” the man said with a sigh. “Let me try to explain it better. With the extra money you make by selling more tacos, you could buy a building on Central Avenue and start a restaurant. You would have seating for hundreds of people. Hungry customers would come from miles and miles around just to eat your delicious food.”

The man in the suit talked faster and faster.

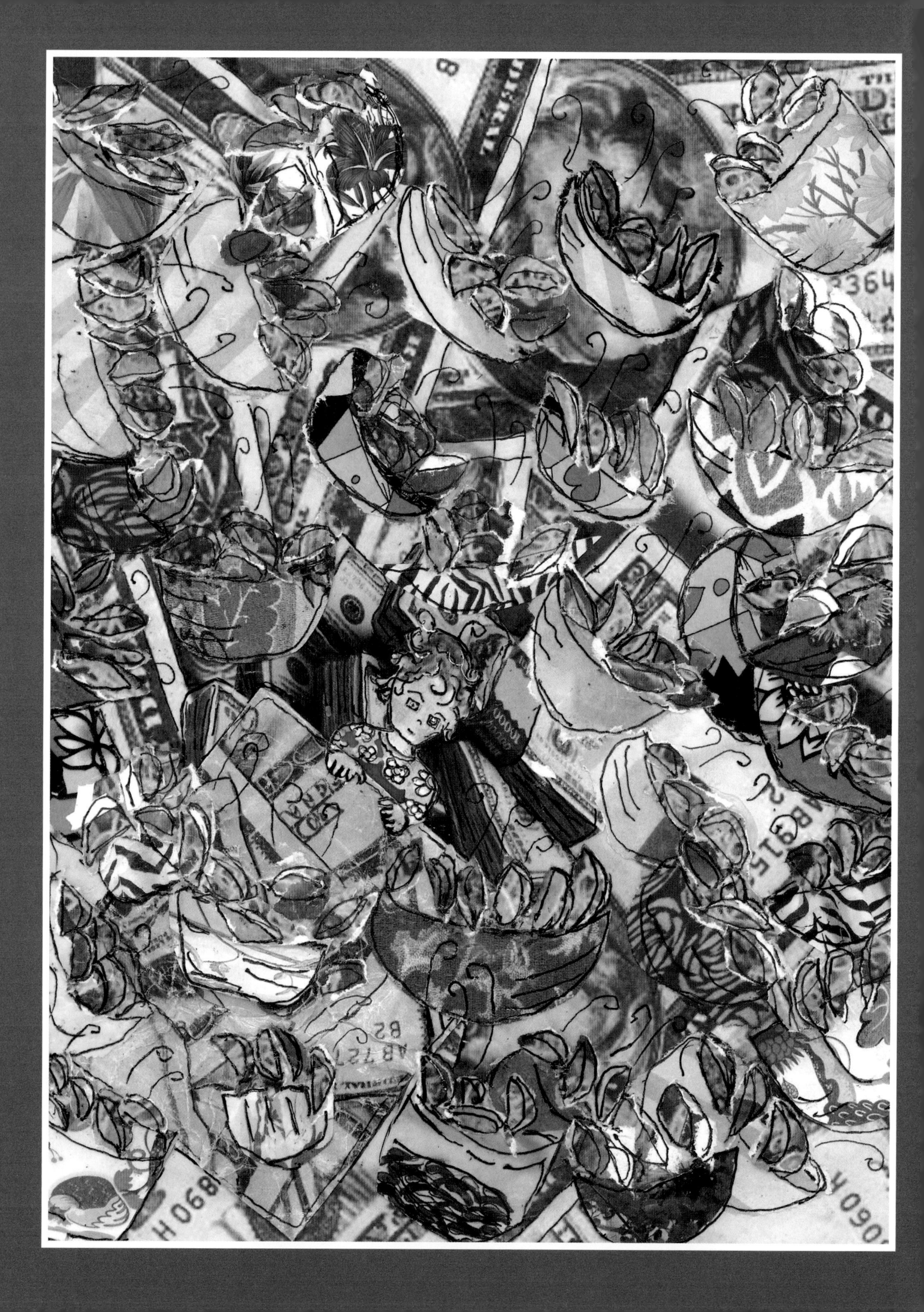

"Of course, in order to cook for so many hungry people, you will have to make tacos all day long. You will not have a minute to spare. There will be no more wasting time sitting on the porch and watching the boys play ball. No more time to cook a Mexican feast every evening. You will be cooking all day and all night for your customers."

The man's eyes almost sparkled. "I can see it now," he said. "We will be swimming in money!"

"Señor, I do love to cook," Isabel replied in a soft, calm voice. "But I cook because it makes me happy. I like to see people enjoy my food. I don't cook to make money so that I can buy more things. What would I possibly do then?"

The man in the black suit barely paused for a breath. "Well, I was hoping you would ask me that! When the money rolls in, that's when the real magic begins," he almost shouted. "FRANCHISING, my dear, FRANCHISING! We will open up restaurants all over the country!"

"Excuse me, Señor, but that sounds like quite a lot of cooking. Remember, it's just me and my one little pot," said Isabel.

The man in the black suit leaned back in his chair. He chuckled to himself as his bulging belly jiggled up and down.

He said, "Little lady, you won't have to cook at all anymore. No more sweating in the kitchen for you. You will be a MANAGER. You will have employees to train. You will be the big boss, cracking the whip."

The table creaked as the man in the suit leaned in close. His lips curled into a sly little smile. Believe it or not, he talked even faster.

"We will expand with restaurants in cities all across the country. You will live in New York City. You'll have diamonds and pearls and fancy cars. You'll have to travel all the time, so I recommend flying in your own private jet. You will be The Queen of Tacos," he almost shouted.

"Of course, you won't get to see your family much. But the money will be worth it! We will be rich!"

The man in the suit laughed again, long and loud, as bits of taco sprayed from his mouth across the table.

Isabel quietly began to clear the table of now-empty dishes. Very softly she asked, "Then what, Señor? What would I do next?"

"Then what?" the man in the suit bellowed. "Well, here's what you could do next. After years and years of work, you could move back to Arizona with your family and friends. You could get up early and sip your coffee as you watch the Arizona sunrise. You could make breakfast for Poncho and the boys. In the afternoon you could sit on the porch and watch them play ball in the yard.

"At sunset, you all could sing as Poncho plays the guitar. And you could cook a feast for your family and friends. You could eat, drink, tell stories, and laugh together late into the night," he said, finally running out of breath.

Isabel, Poncho, and the boys thanked the man in the black suit. They shook his hand, walked him out front to his fancy black car, and wished him a good night. Isabel had much to think about as they went back inside.

That night, Isabel tucked the boys into bed. She kissed them each on the cheek and said goodnight. At their door she turned off the light and took a long look at her beautiful family.

A lovely smile spread across Isabel's face. She knew EXACTLY what she wanted to do the next morning ... and every single morning after that.

Isabel was awake before dawn. She sat in her kitchen and sipped her coffee as she watched another beautiful Arizona sunrise. Soon, she would start cooking a delicious breakfast for her family....

# AFTERWORD

After raising their two sons George and Ralph, Isabel and Poncho opened a takeout in a little house on Central Avenue in Phoenix, Arizona in 1972 and named it Ponchos Mexican Food. They lived in the back of the house and served Isabel's delicious food out of the front of the house. As word spread, they moved out of the home, converting it into a full-service restaurant that is still successful today. In 1999, President Bill Clinton made a surprise visit and enjoyed dinner at Ponchos.

Slow-cooked meats, flavorful sauces, fresh seasonal vegetables, and homemade salsas wrapped in warm, handmade tortillas proved a hit from the very beginning. There is no substitute for the delicate flavors and aromas of the family recipes.

In 1986, Isabel and Poncho's son, George, and his wife, Mary, opened the first Someburros, quickly gaining a loyal clientele of diners who, generation after generation, returned again and again, craving the restaurant's signature dishes and warm atmosphere.

More recently, George and Mary's children—Tim, Amy, and Jennilyn—have taken over the daily operations of Someburros. Even young grandson Cody Vasquez has become skilled at whipping up the family's inspired cuisine on his own, continuing to set the tone for younger generations to experience Someburros' made-from-scratch specialties.

In 2013, The Vasquez Family opened Isabel's Amor in Gilbert, Arizona, dedicated to serving more of Isabel's signature dishes that were uncovered in an old, tattered recipe book. Next to the bar, black and white photos are displayed on the wall of Isabel and her family as Poncho's old cowboy hat hangs for all to see.

Isabel passed away just two months before Someburros opened in 1986, but her legacy lives on in the delicious food, bringing smiles to the faces of hungry families every day.

# GLOSSARY

## Tasty Mexican Food Terms to Learn

**Adobo:** a sauce made with chiles, garlic, vinegar, onions, and tomatoes

**Adobado:** meat flavored with Adobo

**Ajo:** garlic

**Al pastor:** marinated pork

**Albóndigas:** meatballs with rice in broth, often with vegetables

**Ancho:** dried poblano chile pepper

**Arroz:** rice

**Barbacoa:** barbecue

**Bistec:** beefsteak

**Buñuelo:** a thin fried pastry finished with a sweet topping

**Burro/Burrito:** a large flour tortilla filled with meat, cheese, or beans

**Calabaza:** squash

**Camarón:** shrimp

**Carne asada:** grilled, thin-cut beef

**Carnitas:** a dish made with small pieces of shredded, fried pork

**Chalupa:** thick, boat-shaped corn tortilla fried and stuffed with ingredients

**Charro beans:** pinto beans simmered with bacon, onions, and tomatoes

**Chicharrones:** deep fried pork rinds

**Chilaquiles:** fried tortillas, usually topped with salsa or mole and cheese

**Chimichanga:** deep fried, meat-filled burrito

**Chipotle:** dried, smoked jalapeño chiles

**Chorizo:** Mexican sausage made with ground pork and spicy seasonings

**Chile con queso:** melted cheese dip flavored with mild green chiles

**Chile relleno:** stuffed green chile peppers battered with egg and fried

**Enchilada:** tortilla dipped in chile sauce, filled with meat or cheese, rolled up, and baked, usually served topped with salsa and cheese

**Ensalada:** salad

**Fajitas:** sizzling meat (chicken or beef) served on a platter with tortillas and condiments served on the side

**Flan:** rich custard dessert with layer of soft caramel on top

**Flauta:** small, flute-shaped corn tortilla stuffed with chicken or beef, sealed, and deep-fried until crisp

**Gordito:** taco with a thick-shelled tortilla

**Guacamole:** dish made from mashed avocado and lime or lemon juice, usually containing onions, chiles, and other seasonings

**Habanero:** extremely hot chile pepper

**Horchata:** refreshing drink made with rice milk and cinnamon

**Huevos:** eggs

**Jalapeño:** medium-hot green chile pepper

**Queso:** melted cheese

**Machaca:** spicy dried beef marinated with onions and peppers

**Mariscos:** shellfish

**Masa:** dough made from dried corn

**Menudo:** spicy soup made with tripe

**Mole:** spicy, rich sauce made with nuts, seeds, chiles, and chocolate

**Nachos:** crisp tortilla chips topped with melted cheese and chopped chiles, invented in 1943 by Ignacio "Nacho" Anaya in Piedras Negras, Mexico

**Pepitas:** roasted pumpkin seeds

**Pescado:** fish

**Picante:** spicy hot sauce

**Pico de Gallo:** relish of fresh tomatoes, onions, and chile peppers

**Poblano:** large, mild, green chile pepper

**Pollo:** chicken

**Pollo asado:** chicken marinated in citrus or vinegar

**Pozole:** soup or stew made with hominy, pork, chile, and vegetables

**Puerco:** pork

**Quesadilla:** flour tortilla filled with cheese, folded in half, and toasted

**Ranchero sauce:** spicy, tomato-based sauce with onions and green chiles

**Refried beans:** smoked red or pinto beans that are mashed then fried

**Salsa:** spicy tomato-based sauce used as a dip with chips or accent dishes

**Taco:** soft or hard corn tortilla filled with meat, cheese, or beans

**Tamale:** corn masa filled with pork, beef or corn, usually steamed in corn husks

**Torta:** sandwich made with meat, sauce, avocado, and tomato

# About Tim S. Vasquez

## Author

**Husband. Father. Coach. Entrepreneur. Philanthropist. Part-time Wordsmith.**

Tim S. Vasquez's casual, easy-to-read writing style has collided with his vast life experiences to create his long-awaited first book, *The Taco Stand*. Growing up in the kitchen of his parents' Mexican restaurant in Tempe, Arizona has provided him the impetus for the book. Tim is the owner and operator of his family's restaurants, Someburros and Isabel's Amor, where he strives each and every day to honor the legacy of his Nana Isabel and Tata Poncho.

Tim's love of baseball and working with young children led him to host free baseball clinics for the underprivileged boys and girls of Guadalupe, Arizona, where his family has deep roots. That is what sparked his passion for giving back. A portion of the proceeds from this book will be donated to Frank Elementary School in Guadalupe to give children who come from humble beginnings the ability to rise up, succeed, and even pay it forward someday.

**Twitter: @timmyv1993**
**Instagram: @timmyv93**

# About Linda Kay Ost

*Illustrator*

## The Art Process

The illustrations in this book were created using watercolors, pens, and love (secret ingredient… shh!)

## The Artist

All I want to do is create art! I am head-over-heels in love with using and crafting innovative artistic methods. I have always resisted rules, structure, and instructions; instead opting for chance and "Let's just see what happens!" I am fearless when it comes to new ways of expressing myself and am often seen searching for objects such as bottle caps, bolts, and wires to fashion into new experiments of color, texture, and meaning.

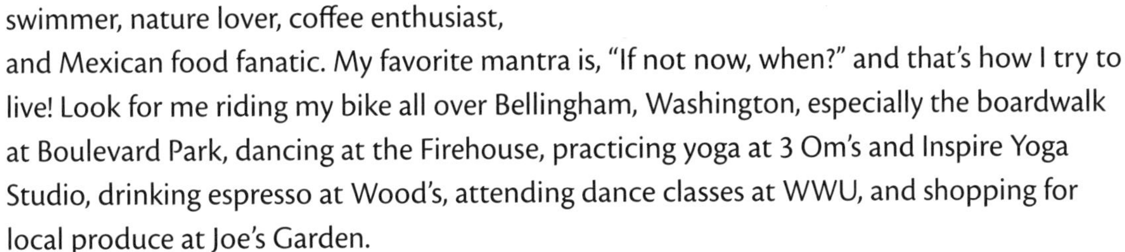

I am a mama, grandma, yogi, dancer, swimmer, nature lover, coffee enthusiast, and Mexican food fanatic. My favorite mantra is, "If not now, when?" and that's how I try to live! Look for me riding my bike all over Bellingham, Washington, especially the boardwalk at Boulevard Park, dancing at the Firehouse, practicing yoga at 3 Om's and Inspire Yoga Studio, drinking espresso at Wood's, attending dance classes at WWU, and shopping for local produce at Joe's Garden.

**Facebook: @lindakayost**

# ABOUT STORY MONSTERS LLC

Story Monsters LLC is home to the award-winning Story Monsters Ink® magazine, the literary resource for teachers, librarians, and parents—selected by *School Library Journal* as one of the best magazines for kid and teens.

We also support authors of all stages to strive for excellence through our award-winning book production and marketing services, Dragonfly Book Awards contests, Story Monsters Approved! program, and opportunities to connect with schools and the media at AuthorBookings.com.

**www.storymonsters.com**

**Facebook: @storymonsters**